This Book Belongs to:

Mickey's Young Readers Library

VOLUME

1
Mickey's Birthday Surprise

STORY BY MARY PACKARD

Activities by Thoburn Educational Enterprises, Inc.

A BANTAM BOOK
NEW YORK · TORONTO · LONDON · SYDNEY · AUCKLAND

Mickey's Birthday Surprise   A Bantam Book/September 1990. All rights reserved. © 1990 The Walt Disney Company. Developed by
The Walt Disney Company in conjunction with Nancy Hall, Inc. This book may not be reproduced or transmitted in any form or by any means.
ISBN 0–553–05614–X
Published simultaneously in the United States and Canada. Bantam Books are published by Bantam Doubleday Dell Publishing Group,
Inc. Its trademark, consisting of the words "Bantam Books" and the portrayal of a rooster, is Registered in U.S. Patent
and Trademark Office and in other countries. Marca Registrada. Bantam Books 666 Fifth Avenue, New York, New York 10103.
Printed in the United States of America
0 9 8 7 6 5 4 3 2 1
A Walt Disney BOOK FOR YOUNG READERS

One day, Pluto and Mickey's kitten, Molly, watched as Mickey busied himself around the kitchen. Mickey set the table. He put a big plate of cookies and another big plate of brownies right in the middle of the table. Then he made a big pitcher of lemonade.

"We are having guests," Molly thought happily. "I wonder who's coming to visit," thought Pluto. Mickey noticed how Pluto and Molly kept looking at the food on the table. "Why don't you two play outside until our guests come," Mickey suggested. He gently shooed them out the door.

Outside, Pluto ran over to the mailbox. Molly
followed. Pluto saw a box sitting beside the mailbox.
He sniffed it, but he couldn't tell what was inside.
Molly brushed up against it. It didn't feel like much
of anything to her. Pluto decided to bring it in to
Mickey. Then they would find out what was inside.

Pluto brought Mickey the box and laid it at Mickey's feet.

"Why thank you, Pluto!" Mickey exclaimed. "Grandma Duck has mailed a birthday present to me! Today is my birthday, you know!"

Then Mickey tore off the wrapping and the ribbon.

"What fun I'll have with those!" Molly thought, as she watched Mickey throw away the paper and ribbon.

Then Mickey opened the box. "Oh, boy!" he cried. "It's a toy kitten. What a pretty little thing she is, too. And just look at that beautiful shiny collar."

Mickey saw a little windup key on the kitten's side.

"Maybe it's a music box," Mickey said as he turned the key. He set the toy down. Sure enough, it began to play a lovely tune. Then, much to Mickey's surprise, the toy kitten began to dance around the room. Around and around it twirled, clapping its paws and mewing softly.

"Isn't that cute?" Mickey exclaimed.

Pluto wagged his tail. But the toy kitten scared Molly. She arched her back and fluffed out her fur. Then she let out a loud hiss to let the toy know who was boss.

"Silly, Molly," Mickey said. "Don't you know that a toy kitty won't hurt you?"

When the music stopped, Mickey left the toy kitten on the floor while he dusted the tables, and shook out the rug.

Pluto forgot about the toy kitten. He went to take a nap.

Molly crept over to the toy. She was curious. She wanted to see it dance again. She gave it a pat. But it would not play. It just fell on its side.

Mickey rushed over. He picked up the toy.

"Be careful, Molly," he said with a frown. "This toy is very special. And I don't want it to break."

Molly felt sad. She hurried over to where Pluto was napping. She curled up beside him and waited for the guests.

In a few minutes, the doorbell rang. Mickey opened the door. Pluto and Molly leaped up from the corner to greet Donald and his nephews.

"Happy birthday!" they sang.

"Come on in," said Mickey happily. Donald followed Mickey. The nephews stayed behind to play with Pluto and Molly.

Pluto found his ball and dropped it at Huey's feet. Dewey and Louie giggled as Molly pounced on the string they had brought her. They were all having a fine time until Donald called out, "Hey, boys. Come in here. Mickey has a new toy." With that, Huey, Dewey, and Louie raced over to play with Mickey's toy kitten, leaving Pluto and Molly behind.

Daisy and Minnie were the next to arrive. Daisy patted Pluto's head while Minnie picked up the kitten to cuddle.

"Thump, thump, thump!" wagged Pluto's tail happily.

"Purr, purr, purr," hummed Molly.

Suddenly the toy kitten came twirling toward them.

"How cute!" cried Minnie. She quickly set Molly on the floor. Then she and Daisy went to play with the new toy.

When Goofy arrived, Molly and Pluto were happy. Goofy always brought Molly and Pluto good treats to eat. Pluto wagged his tail hopefully. But Goofy spotted Mickey's new toy. He headed for the new kitten, forgetting to give Molly and Pluto anything at all.

Pluto looked at Molly. Molly looked at Pluto.
Their feelings were hurt.

"We don't need them to play with anyway,"
Molly's look seemed to say. Then she danced over
to the wastebasket, where Mickey had thrown the
wrapping paper and ribbon. Pluto followed.

Molly pulled out the ribbon and ran with it. Pluto watched with a puzzled grin as Molly played. Soon Molly was all tangled up in the ribbon—and all Pluto could see was Molly's nose, ears, and tail! And there was no way Pluto could untangle Molly!

Just then Mickey noticed the crumpled pile of ribbon—and Molly!

"I'll set you free," said Mickey. He gently pulled the ribbon from her paws and threw it away.

"This time, Molly, leave the ribbon alone and you won't get into trouble," Mickey scolded.

Molly pretended not to listen to Mickey. She licked her paw as though she hadn't heard a word.

After Mickey had gone back to his guests—and
the toy kitten—Molly went over to Pluto. "Let's play
something else together," she seemed to say.

But Pluto had lost interest in Molly's way of
playing. He gave her a little lick and went over to
join the others. After all, Goofy might remember to
give Pluto his treat!

Molly couldn't believe it. Even her friend Pluto had gone over to the other side!

Molly looked around for something else to do. She climbed up on the windowsill and looked outside. To Molly, things seemed more friendly out there.

"I know I'm supposed to stay inside," thought
Molly. "But no one really cares what I do, anyway!"
    With one last look at Pluto, who was busy
watching the toy kitten, Molly jumped down from the
sill into the backyard. She was gone from the yard
in a flash.

In the meantime, Pluto was beginning to get tired of the toy kitten's tricks. It did the same things over and over again—never anything new, like Molly did.

At the thought of Molly, Pluto looked around. "Where was Molly, anyway?" Pluto wondered. He hunted for her in all her favorite places. But he couldn't find her anywhere.

Pluto began to worry about Molly. He went over to Mickey and pushed him a bit—he wanted Mickey to know that Molly was missing. But Mickey didn't understand what Pluto was trying to say. He thought Pluto wanted to play with the new kitten.

"Sorry, Pluto, you can't play with this kitten. It's a very special toy, and it might break. Why don't you go play with Molly instead?"

Then Mickey turned back to the toy kitten again.

It was no use. Pluto knew he would have to find Molly all on his own. Pluto slipped out of the house. He perked up his ears, and he listened very hard. He heard birds. He heard squirrels. But he didn't hear any kitty sounds at all.

He poked his nose behind every bush in the
yard. He looked and he looked. But there was no
sign of Molly. She was nowhere to be found!

Pluto went into the woods in back of Mickey's house. The woods had a lot of very tall trees. All of a sudden, Pluto's ears perked up again. He thought he heard a soft "meow, meow!" from far away. "That sounds like Molly," Pluto thought. So he followed the sound, and the "meows" got louder and louder.

When he heard a "MEOW, MEOW," from above, Pluto looked up. There was Molly.

"How did Molly get all the way up there?" Pluto wondered. "And how is she going to get down?"

It was then Pluto knew he just had to get Mickey.

"I'll be back with help," Pluto barked. "Stay right there!" He ran as fast as he could to Mickey's house.

Pluto raced into the house. By this time, all the guests had gone home. Mickey had just put away the leftover birthday cake when Pluto arrived.

Pluto jumped up on Mickey and began to whine.

"What's wrong, Pluto?" Mickey asked. "Do you want me to follow you somewhere?" Mickey asked.

Pluto barked. "Yes," he seemed to say.

"OK, Pluto—lead the way!" Mickey said.
Mickey followed as Pluto led him quickly through
the woods.

When they got to the tree where Molly was stuck, Pluto stared straight up at the top of the tree and barked.

"Oh my goodness . . . I don't believe it! Don't worry, little kitty—I'll save you!" Mickey called.

"Pluto—you stay here with Molly. I'll be back with a ladder in a jiffy."

In no time at all, Mickey returned with a ladder.
And quick as a wink, Mickey hurried up the ladder
and gently took Molly into his arms. When they
were both safely back on the ground, Pluto gave
Molly a great big kiss.

"Good dog, Pluto," Mickey said. "And you're a good friend, too. A better friend than I've been to you and Molly today."

Molly just gave a tiny "meow." She most certainly agreed!

When they got back home, Mickey gave Molly a dish of milk. He gave Pluto and Molly each a large piece of birthday cake.

Then he put the toy kitten on the table for them all to play with later.

"You know," said Mickey, patting Molly on the head, "no toy kitten could ever be as special as you are. And having you safe and sound is the best birthday present ever."

And Pluto wagged his tail hard (since his mouth was too full to bark). "I agree!" was what he seemed to say.

Think About It

How Did They Feel?

In the beginning of the story, how did Mickey, Pluto, and Molly feel about the new toy kitten? Look at the picture below to help you remember. By the end of the story, how did Mickey feel about the toy kitten? How did he feel about Molly?

True Feelings

See how much of this story you remember. Read the sentences below and tell whether they are true or false. Explain why.

1. Molly loved the toy kitten from the very start.

2. Pluto was surprised to see the toy kitten dance and play music.

3. Mickey was frightened by the toy kitten.

4. All of Mickey's friends were impressed by the toy kitten.

5. The toy kitten loved to drink milk from Molly's bowl.

Fun With Words

Act How You Feel!

Mickey wants to know how you look when you
feel sad, happy, surprised, silly, shy, or worried.
What things can make you feel each way?

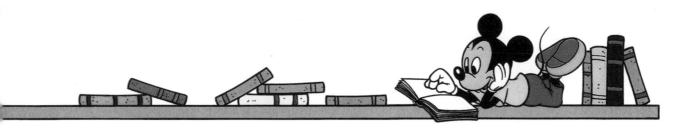

Birthday Wordmaking

How many words can you make from the letters BIRTHDAY SURPRISE? Below are a few words that Mickey has thought of to get you started.